The
Powers

The Powers*

*The Not-so-super Superheroes

Kevin
Stevens

Illustrated by
Sheena Dempsey

Little Island

Suzie

JP

The
Powers

Pucker*

*The dog

The Powers: The Not-so-super Superheroes
Published 2013
by Little Island
7 Kenilworth Park
Dublin 6W
Ireland

www.littleisland.ie
www.readthepowers.com

ISBN 978-1-908195-83-8

Typeset in Georgia (by Matthew Carter), titles in Justy (by Justin Brown) and Minya (by Ray Larabie)

Design by Fidelma Slattery @ Someday.ie

Printed in Poland by Drukarnia Skleniarz

Little Island receives financial assistance from
The Arts Council (An Chomhairle Ealaíon), Dublin, Ireland.

Little Island would like to acknowledge funding we received from Dublin City Council.

Comhairle Cathrach
Bhaile Átha Cliath
Dublin City Council

10 9 8 7 6 5 4 3 3

Visit **www.readthepowers.com** to read Suzie's blog, see the Powers animation and hear the theme tune! Upload your own superhero artwork, download printable activities and learn more about the not-so-super superheroes. They're pooper-soured!

Thanks*

My thanks to the superheroes who brought the world
of the Powers to life: Alice Stevens, master of the
power universe; Sheena Dempsey, wonder illustrator;
Dee Sullivan, shape-shifting blogger; Michael Stevens,
Stratocaster Man; Elaina O'Neill, track of all jades;
and Siobhán Parkinson, who makes the world of
publishing move by telekinesis.

*No animals were harmed in the making of this book.

To my
super
nieces:
Nora,
Anna
and
Lois

1

Smoke
on the
Water

JP rushed into the sitting-room.

'Dad's head's on fire!'

'*Again?*'

Suzie threw her book aside and leapt to her feet. The sharp, crinkly smell of burning hair drifted from the kitchen.

'Fly to Mum,' she told her brother. 'Tell her we need a cloudburst. Inside the house. *Now*.'

Feeling the chaos, Pucker had become a blurred, barking circle, teeth gnashing wildly an inch from his tail.

'Go, JP,' Suzie said. '*Go!*'

He crouched, extended his arms and squeezed shut his eyes.

'*Outside!*' Suzie shouted at him, hands fluttering. 'Take off outside.'

Too late. JP aimed for the open window but took off at an angle and crashed into the wall. His head bashed off the framed front page of *The Irish Times*, hung proudly by their mum five years ago. LOCAL SUPERHEROES RESCUE IRISH ECONOMY. The Powers' first big headline. A week later the economy had plunged into recession.

In a crash of glass and splitting wood, JP fell on top of whirling Pucker. Howls. Flying fur. A painful grinding sound.

Suzie ran into the kitchen. Wide-eyed, their dad was flapping uselessly at his face with a tea towel. Smoke and flame spurted from the top of his head, leaving scorch marks on the ceiling. In his green sweater and tartan trousers he looked like a giant cigarette lighter.

'Aaaargh!' he screamed, but it was his annoyed scream. He wasn't in pain. He liked fire. When he could control it. Twice that summer he had nearly burned the house down.

'The sink, Dad. Stick your head in the sink!'

Ted didn't hear her. Or wouldn't listen. He was not the best listener, even when he wasn't on fire.

'Dad.'

Now he was doing a Pucker, tearing around the room, flailing his arms and shaking his head, making things worse. Actually fanning the flames. Flakes of burning paint dropped from the ceiling. Smoke billowed, thick as tomato soup. It was like a war zone.

In the sitting-room JP threw Pucker aside and brushed himself off. Their mum, where was their mum? Of course – at the garden centre. Where she always was. Two minutes by air. Then he remembered his cape. He could not fly straight without it. Where was it? He stuck his head inside the kitchen door and peered through the smoke.

'Suzie,' he shouted, 'did you cake my tape?'

'Cake your tape?'

'Take my cape.'

'Forget about your cape – go and get Mum!'

All four burners on the stove blazed. The room was like a furnace. This was what happened when their dad tried to light the gas burner with a snap of his fingers. *Zing. Blip. Whoosh.* He thought he was so cool. Afterwards he would wink at the kids and blow smoke from his finger like it was the barrel of a pistol. A gunslinger making a cup of tea. When he wasn't exploding into flames.

JP sprinted away. Using telekinesis, Suzie made Ted slip on the tiled floor and tumble headlong into the kitchen sink. She unleashed the taps, tripled the water flow and bent the stream upwards so that it doused his head and put out the fire.

Eyebrows smouldering, gasping for breath, he staggered back and fell into a kitchen chair.

'Holy smoke,' he said, rubbing his charred chin. 'That came out of nowhere.'

'Oh, really?' Suzie said. 'Like one of Mum's lightning bolts?'

'Suzie, pet, sarcasm doesn't suit you. If you had powers, you'd know how hard they are to control. Would you mind putting on the kettle? I'm as thirsty as a llama.'

Over the sizzling of Ted's hair came the sound of scrabbling claws, a panicky thumping, growls and panting. Pucker exploded through the door, tearing across the kitchen like a squall of rain, slipping and sliding on the wet floor and knocking Suzie's legs from under her, before he squeezed through the pet door and disappeared into the back garden with a strangled howl.

Dazed, Suzie lay on her back while her dad muttered to himself. 'Let's see now: thin flame, low heat, fin-ger SNAP – high heat, super grill, slow hand CLAP. Or is it the other way round?'

Suzie stared at the ceiling. Was that more smoke? Was her dad on fire again? But there was no smell. Was it – it couldn't be – storm clouds?

Suzie scrambled to her feet and looked out the window. Her mum stood on the footpath, clutching a bag of peat moss and holding a new spade over her shoulder like a rifle. JP was beside her, pointing at the house and jerking his head like a puppet. His clothes were torn, and bits of wood and glass clung to his hair.

'It's out,' Suzie yelled. 'The fire's out!'

But her mum couldn't hear her through the double glazing, and she had that funny look on her face that meant she was bringing on the weather. *Let it be a sprinkle*, Suzie commanded, but she couldn't get her weather-resistance power going in time.

Blinding rain. An enormous crack of thunder. And then a ragged spear of lightning lit up the kitchen like dynamite and blew Ted's sweater off.

Head wobbling, he blinked at Suzie and brushed burning fibres of fabric from his chest. His hissing hair stood up in soaked spikes. The rain spilled over the appliances, dripped off the counters, splashed onto the floor, where teacups floated like little boats.

'I take it that's your mother outside,' he said.

Suzie nodded, wringing water from her sopping clothes.

'Well,' he said, 'we'd better get changed. It looks like the chipper for dinner.'

2

The
Power
of Love

Ted and Clare had been warned. But love is stronger than any superpower.

They had met at the Dark Knights Super Daze convention in London. This was back in the 1990s, when Ireland's only known superhero was a leprechaun named Myles whose power was the ability to pick winners at the races. He was soon barred from every racecourse and betting shop in the country. But by then he was rolling in gold, and he retired to Florida, where he married a weather woman from Fox News and grew fat and lazy.

'And not once,' said Ted darkly, whenever he spoke of Myles, 'did he exercise his power for the good of the country.'

Clare had been talking to Wonder Woman at the Astral Projection booth when Ted walked by. He heard her Dublin accent and waited for her. At least that was how he told it. Clare would later claim that he had been smitten by Wonder Woman.

'You're the one who smited me,' Ted would counter.

'Smote.'

'Smote?'

'Smite, smote, smitten.'

'I'm the pup and you're the kitten.'

'Don't be talking nonsense.'

'Is it nonsense to say that Wonder Woman doesn't hold a candle to you?' Ted demanded.

'You held a candle to her.'

A candle? More like a blowtorch. So flustered was Ted when Clare first spoke to him that flames shot out the cuffs of his duffel coat and lit Wonder Woman's cape on fire. When Clare had tried to generate a localised rain storm, her temperature control went wonky and the Warrior Princess of the Amazons was frozen in a solid block of ice.

It was a scandal. They were barred from the exhibitors' hall.

And officially warned.

It was written, clear as kryptonite, in the by-laws of the International Superhero Association: 'Emotional involvement of heroes with mutually contraindicative powers is banned without exception under penalty of expulsion from the association and suspension of all superheroic privileges.'

Mutually contraindicative. A fancy way of saying their powers went ballistic when Ted and Clare were together. They should not get involved. Or get married. And children? Don't even think about it. Who knew how they'd turn out?

But what could the two of them do? Love was in the air – as well as flames like Hallowe'en bonfires and great jagged flashes of lightning and hailstones the size of grapefruit. And that was just when they looked at each other.

They married a month later in Dublin City Hall. When Ted kissed the bride, the thermometer hit forty and the wedding flowers drooped on their stalks. They honeymooned in Gotham City (Batman refused to meet them – he was treasurer of the association) and two weeks later moved into a semi-detached house in Castlerock. An average couple in an average Dublin neighbourhood.

Well, not exactly. Oh, if their neighbours only knew what was in store! The flash floods. The burning trees. The County Council van swallowed by a giant crack in the road.

'We have a responsibility,' Ted said from the start.

'You can't be handed such a gift,' Clare said, 'without giving back.'

So they gave back. Or tried to. True, they had been suspended by the association. But they lived in Ireland, where superhero laws were fuzzy, to say the least. Or ignored.

Those early stories were now part of family history. The time the Irish football team played Spain in the World Cup, and Clare sent a puff of wind to help a Damien Duff shot towards goal. The wind went the wrong way and pushed the ball away from goal. Ireland lost on penalties.

Or the snowstorm of 2004. Ted was walking down O'Connell Street in his green-check lumberman jacket and fire-engine-red wellingtons when he saw a minibus full of schoolchildren sliding on the icy road and heading towards the Liffey. On came the afterburners and a super-whoosh of flame. The ice melted and the children were saved, but Ted had trouble turning off the fire and reduced the brand-new Dublin Spire to a mound of molten stainless steel. Cost to rebuild: five million euro. Angry shouting in the chamber of Dublin City Council: priceless.

The economy, the banks, the summers of endless rain. Was it the Powers' fault? They didn't think so. The country begged to differ.

When Suzie was born her parents counted her fingers and toes and watched her day and night for signs of strange behaviour. But she was perfect. And as far as they could tell, she had no powers. Two years later JP arrived. Another bundle of joy, though he did tend to sleep above the covers – a metre above.

After the Spire incident the Gardaí sent a representative to Castlerock with a message for the Powers: 'Thank you so much for the help. We appreciate it. We really do. But could you please leave civic control and crime-fighting to the police? That's what we're paid for.'

Ted and Clare nodded and smiled and said, 'Of course,' but when the guard was gone they shook their heads.

'How can we expect them to understand?' Ted said. 'They're normal.'

'We're the Powers.'

'We're super.'

'Super-powered.'

But they did their best to be good citizens. They ignored their powers for a while and concentrated on raising the children. Suzie played with her stuffed animals, wrote fairy tales and had imaginary friends. Started school. Liked to read. No flames. No thunderstorms.

And JP? Well, when he was distracted he might float in the air like a day-old balloon, but a gentle push and he was back to earth. They just needed to keep an eye on him. And everything was fine. Until his first day in junior infants.

His proud parents brought him to Castlerock Primary School, just as they had with Suzie. He looked so cute in his grey trousers, bottle-green sweater and striped tie. Their little man. His hair sticking up at the back, as it always had. A faraway look on his face, as if he was dreaming he was a bird soaring among the thin clouds high above the earth.

Until Ted and Clare hugged him and said goodbye.

And it dawned on JP that they were going to leave him there. By himself. All alone. When he had never been away from his parents. Ever.

He cried. He screamed. Ted and Clare felt miserable. They tore his hand from their grasp and handed him over to the teacher. They walked away from the classroom, almost crying themselves. It had not been like this with Suzie. She had loved going to school. Couldn't wait to get out of the house. But poor little JP. How would he manage?

They reached the car and stood in the street, unable to leave. Back in the classroom, JP had stopped crying, but something was happening inside him. Some roiling, churning, bubbling centre of energy that made him feel as if he was going to explode. His legs started to tremble and his arms to flap, as if with a life of their own. His teacher frowned. There was a rumbling sound.

Ping, boing, zoom. Off he went like a shot off a shovel, bouncing off ceiling, blackboard, desktop, and through the classroom window with a star-burst of glass, flying skyward at a forty-five-degree angle as Ted and Clare looked up from below, open-mouthed. There was a loud boom as he broke the sound barrier and swept across the sky in a wide curve and headed back towards the school. And downwards. Towards the car. At a thousand miles an hour.

Clare had no choice. They needed deep water. Now. And nothing is as powerful as a mother

concerned for her child. The heavens opened. What took the Bible forty days Clare produced in five seconds, and JP landed with a big splash and floated into his mother's arms, no worse for wear.

Of course, the neighbourhood didn't look too good after the flood, especially when Ted tried to dry out the school and burned it down. The children cheered and headed home, but the principal wasn't pleased.

From that day on, the lid was off. Now they were a superhero family.

3

Hit the Road, Jack

Ted had destroyed the kitchen once too often. And now he claimed it was *Clare* who had destroyed it. So she led him out to her beloved garden and sat him on the bench beneath the maple tree. It was her 'time out' corner, where she sent the children when they were bold.

'You're under stress,' she said.

'No, I'm not.'

With his eyebrows burned off he looked forever surprised. His head was wrapped in a bandage. As he spoke, curls of smoke puffed from his ears.

'You need a break,' Clare said. 'We all do. A break from Dublin. From being super.'

'I told you we should have replaced that cooker.'

An occasional thumping echoed from above. Pucker snuffled in the bushes, searching for a cat or bird or fox that he would never catch.

'It's not the cooker, Ted. Let's go to West Cork. Anna is always saying we can use their caravan in Baltimore.'

'You mean where that famous gold cross was stolen!'

'Ted, for a *holiday*. Besides, those gold treasures have been stolen from museums all over the country, not just from Baltimore.'

'But we could catch that gang.'

'That's not what the guards think. Remember when you roasted that famous archaeologist?'

'How was I to know he wasn't stealing that chalice?'

'He's the director of the National Museum!'

Ted shook his head and tugged at his bandage. 'The nation depends on us, Clare.'

'The nation can do without us for a week.'

'And what about your garden?'

'I've thought of that. I'll set the weather for the time we're away. Every day will be a perfect mix of steady sunshine and ten minutes of rainfall.'

A scream of frustration came from the house. Suzie burst through the sliding doors and stomped across the lawn.

'I'm upstairs,' she wailed. 'At my desk. Trying to study. And JP is practising flying. In his room.'

'I wondered where that unholy banging was coming from,' Ted said.

Clare raised her hand like a lollipop lady. 'Hang on a minute, Suzie. Study? School's been out for two weeks.'

Suzie set her hands on her hips. Put on her righteous face. 'Well, school wouldn't have closed early if someone hadn't insisted on lighting the barbecue on sports day –'

'That place was a fire hazard,' Ted shouted.

'Now let's not get into all that again,' Clare said. 'So the classrooms won't be rebuilt until September. The same thing happened to JP's school and that turned out fine.'

'But *I'm* going into secondary school in September, and it's a big change, and Fiona told me what books I have to read for first year, and it's very competitive, I want to be prepared, and ...'

She stopped talking, out of breath. From the first floor of the house came a dull, steady pounding. Pucker tumbled from the hedge, leaves in his ears, frantically scratching his ribs and howling.

Ted and Clare looked at each other.

'You're right,' Ted said. 'We need a holiday.'

The family car was a ten-year-old Ford Fiasco that Ted refused to trade in. It had a dodgy clutch, flapping fan belts, a broken exhaust and a leaky fuel line. But he loved that car. He didn't even mind when it broke down.

Which it did as soon as they were on the M50.

Ted whistled and popped the bonnet and said things like 'must be the solenoid' and 'carburettor's dirty again'. Clare got out and stood in the hard shoulder with her arms folded. She stared at the steaming engine while Ted rooted through the boot. Traffic whizzed past. JP was under strict orders to stay in the car. Suzie's ears were plugged with headphones and her nose was in a book. On the seat between them Pucker squirmed and whimpered.

'I thought we had warning flares back here,' Ted said.

'We don't need flares. It's broad daylight.'

'I could always ...'

He made as if to snap his fingers.

'No. Call the AA.'

'I think I might have ... well, you know, let our membership lapse.'

Now Clare was steaming. JP stuck his head out the window. 'I have to go to the toilet.'

'Stay right where you are.'

'I *really* have to go.'

Pucker's whimper had grown to a growl.

'What did I tell you before we left the house?'

'I didn't have to go at the house.'

Ted took a spanner from the boot and went to work. In ten minutes he had the engine ticking over. At least for the moment.

As he closed the bonnet, a Garda car pulled up behind them, blue lights flashing. Two guards stepped out, putting on their hats and tugging at their utility belts.

The one who had been driving spoke. 'Everything all right here, lads?'

'Not a bother, guard,' Ted said, wiping his oily hands on a rag. 'Everything's sorted. I know this car like the back of my head.'

The second guard squinted at Ted. The head bandage. The toasted face. 'Aren't you –?'

'Ted Power, yes, that's me.'

A look of deep concern fell across the faces of the guards.

'And this is my wife, Clare,' Ted continued. 'I'm sure you know all about her as well, but I have to tell you, guards, don't be looking for any help from us today, nothing super, no way, because we are –' he cleared his throat and spoke loudly so that Clare would hear above the roar of traffic, '– on our holidays.'

But the guards didn't hear a word because they were staring at the back window of the car, where Pucker's writhing face was mashed against the glass. His teeth were bared and his eyes were furious and his big red mouth was dripping saliva, trying to work itself into a howl.

Pucker, you see, hated anyone in a uniform. Postmen, nurses, firefighters, soldiers, guards. Especially guards.

'Is that animal on a lead?' the first guard said, slowly backing away.

'Who, Pucker? Ah, you needn't worry about that little pooch,' Ted said. 'He's as gentle as a ram.'

The Fiasco rocked from side to side. Suddenly Pucker leapt out of the window and onto the roadway, his short legs a blur of motion. The guards legged it back to their car, slamming shut the doors just ahead of Pucker's snapping jaws.

'Pucker!' Ted shouted. 'Pucker! Come here, boy.'

But Pucker's momentum bounced him off the door of the Garda car and onto the busy motorway. JP screamed. The rush-hour traffic swerved. Horns blared. The more Pucker tried to leap clear, the more he put himself in harm's way. But by some miracle every careering car missed him. They went sliding this way and that, tyres screeching, engines revving. Some rebounded off the guard rail. Some of them turned completely around. Others spilled into the ditch. But none of them hit Pucker.

And then the pile-up. It had to happen. A chain reaction – *bang, bang, bang.* One car into another. Smoke everywhere. Broken glass. The crunch of bumpers and the hiss of exploding airbags.

But another miracle: no one was hurt. Not the tiniest scratch. Because the second before each car hit the pile, it slowed mysteriously – just enough so that the drivers and their passengers only got a mild bump. Plenty of damaged cars. But no human injuries. And one unscratched mutt, who barked and capered and had no idea just how close he had come to doggie heaven.

And in the back seat, Suzie, headphones off, her book on her lap, was concentrating as fiercely as she ever had. Telekinesis was hard enough, but when you had to apply it instantly to multiple large objects hurtling down the motorway at a hundred and twenty kilometres an hour – well, it wasn't easy.

Ted closed the boot, got Pucker back in the car, let JP do a wee in the bushes and waved goodbye to the guards, who had ventured out of their car and were surveying the wreckage. Dense smoke. The smell of burning rubber. Rivers of radiator fluid. People stood on the roadway, shaking their heads in amazement.

In twenty minutes the Powers were past the carnage and on their way again.

His good mood rescued, Ted whistled out of tune. 'Well, that worked out in the end,' he said, 'didn't it?'

'And we didn't even have to use our powers,' Clare said.

Suzie turned up the volume on her iPod and started a new chapter of her book.

4

Good
Day
Sunshine

The Powers had never been to West Cork, and arriving in Baltimore was like discovering a secret hiding place. The oak trees, puffy as clouds, arched over the narrow roads, creating long tunnels of cool green. Sunlight flashed on shops and pubs painted red and orange and purple.

Sleepy-headed sheep stared from behind stone walls. And beyond the fields, at the bottom of twisting lanes, were gurgling streams and hidden coves and beaches blanketed with sand so fine it ran through your hands like water.

Like two children in a painting, Suzie and JP stood on the edge of the town harbour. The sea stretched before them like a giant quilt. Pucker panted at their feet. Shading their eyes, they stared at the horizon as the sun slowly dipped towards the Atlantic Ocean. The sunlight broke the glazed surface of the water into a million sparkling pieces. Sailing boats bobbed. Seals and dolphins glided past. The water lapped gently against the harbour walls. In the mild salty air gulls and curlews wheeled and cried.

'This is brilliant,' Suzie said.

The kids had gone exploring while Ted and Clare moved the holiday gear from the car into the caravan. Their parents were not in a good mood. The Fiasco had collapsed four more times on the trip from Dublin, and each breakdown took longer for Ted to fix. By the end he was so annoyed it was dangerous. He nearly burst into flames in a petrol station. And the more Clare told him to cool down, the more they both got hot under the collar. Sparks were flying. Literally.

Baltimore was like a village out of a story-book. Holiday homes glittering in the sunshine. Thatched cottages and patchwork fields. Horses racing along the strand. The caravan was at the far end of town, tucked away in a cove of its own with wooden steps to the beach and a gorgeous little patio where they could eat breakfast in the open air and gaze at Sherkin Island across the turquoise water.

'We'd better go back,' Suzie said. 'Dad and Mum are probably wondering where we are.'

'Look at that bird.'

A large white seabird with black-tipped wings swooped from on high, skimmed the surface of the sea and settled on a distant rock with a neat turn and a flap that JP could only ever dream of doing.

'See what he just did?'

'JP, we're on holiday.'

'I know, I know. No powers.'

A deep voice sounded behind them. 'A gannet,' it said, pronouncing the word as if it had been clipped at the end with a scissors.

The children turned and saw the voice's owner – a tall man in a white yachting cap, blue blazer, flannel trousers and deck shoes. He stood regally with his hands behind his back and his nose in the air.

'*Morus bassanus*,' the man continued. 'A beautiful bird, close relative of the brown booby and, as you quite rightly observe, young man, a spectacular flyer.'

The gold buttons on the man's blazer glinted in the sun. Pucker barked, a bark with a question mark, as if he couldn't tell if this man's fancy clothes were a uniform or not.

'Visiting our lovely little haven?' the man said, leaning down and ruffling Pucker's fur. The dog growled.

'Yes,' Suzie said warily, 'we've just arrived. With our parents. Who are expecting us back. Any time now.'

'Then far be it from me to keep you. But before you go, may I make a recommendation?'

He turned and pointed at a man at the other end of the harbour who was sifting brochures in a leather bag balanced on a marine bollard. The man was short and red-faced, with a scraggly grey beard. He was dressed, in spite of the warm weather, in a knitted cap and heavy fisherman's sweater.

'Do you see that man in the jumper?'

'Uh … yeah.'

'Fits you.'

'The jumper?' JP said. 'That's way too big for me.'

'No. Fits you.' He shouted at the man. 'Fitzhugh! Come here.'

Fitzhugh shuffled over, clutching a handful of brochures. He had a nose like a pomegranate and eyebrows like the ears of a terrier.

'The brochures,' the tall man said impatiently.

'Have 'em here, Mr Beasley, here in the bag, just like you asked.' He gave one each to the kids. On the front of each folded handout was a coloured drawing of a skull and crossbones.

'The World-Famous Museum of Pirates and Buccaneers,' Mr Beasley read from the brochure, his voice like a ringmaster's. 'Right here in Baltimore. Treasure, the jolly roger, cut-throat barbarity, white slavery. It all happened here in this little village. And no better place to learn all about it than in our little museum.'

'Cool,' JP said.

'Thank you very much,' said Suzie, 'but our parents are expecting us.'

'Oh, I'm not suggesting you visit now. We're closed for the day. But do come tomorrow. Or Friday. We are open from nine to six.'

Suzie nudged JP to get him going and herded him along the harbour wall.

'Tell your parents,' Mr Beasley shouted after them. 'They'll love it as much as you will!'

He watched them as they walked around the harbour and past the marina. He leaned close to Fitzhugh. 'You planted the map in the caravan?' he asked.

'I did.'

Beasley smiled, revealing a gold tooth as shiny as his buttons. 'Well,' he drawled, 'perhaps you're not completely worthless after all, Fitzhugh.'

'Uh-oh,' Suzie said.

'What?'

'Look.'

Suzie and JP were walking along the pier road, Pucker at their heels. Ahead, Clare was standing beside the car, which Ted had parked in the shade of a giant pine tree. A dense black cloud floated above the scene, obscuring the top of the tree, rumbling faintly and crackling with orange light.

'I thought Dad was the one losing control,' JP said.

'Not any more.'

Around the car, like toys thrown out of a cot, were tennis rackets, runners, red swimming togs, sandals, boxes of tissues, a broken fishing rod, a torn shirt and three squashed bananas. Ted had his head in the boot and Clare stood behind him, her hands on her hips, scowling and looking ready to kick him in the bum.

Hesitantly, the children entered her force field.

'Where have you two been?'

'We met a pirate,' JP said.

'We did not. We met a creepy man who told us about a pirate museum.'

'Can we go, Mum, can we go?'

'Nobody's going anywhere,' Clare said, 'until we get this car unpacked – properly – and everything put in its rightful place in the caravan.'

Ted's head emerged from the boot. His bandage had slipped so that it covered one ear. 'Has anyone seen your mother's gardening bag? The one with the paisley gloves and new trowel and –'

'Never mind, Ted. You obviously left it behind.'

'I distinctly remember putting it in the boot.'

'Then where is it?'

'Relax, Clare. You don't see me getting upset about the fishing rod, do you?'

'Don't tell me to relax. You broke the fishing rod. And you forgot to pack my gardening gear. Not to mention that the children are traipsing who-knows-where without telling us, the front garden here is like a rubbish tip, and now,' she shouted, glaring at the cloud over her head, 'it looks like it's going to pour rain.'

JP piped up. 'But that's because you –'

'Quiet, JP,' Suzie said.

There was a crack of thunder. The pine tree swayed in the wind. Clare glared. 'What do you have to say for yourselves?'

Before Suzie could stop him, JP said, 'Can we go to the pirate museum tomorrow?'

Clare exploded. 'I'm fed up with the pair of you. Fed up! Both of you – go to your rooms!'

The kids looked at each other. 'How can we go to our rooms,' Suzie said, 'when we haven't even been inside the caravan yet?'

'Aaaaargh!'

Clare stalked into the caravan. The clouds shifted so that they were above the caravan and sheets of lightning flickered over the cove beyond.

Ted watched her until she was inside and then turned to the kids. 'So what's this about a pirate museum?'

5

Hound
Dog

'Dad – look what I found!'

JP came shooting out of his room and tripped on the metal threshold. He fell hard, but before he hit the floor he went into fly mode without thinking. He managed to zoom upside-down beneath the table, but his belt buckle caught the edge of the tablecloth as he buzzed past, sending cutlery, plates, boiled eggs and brown bread scattering to the corners of the kitchen. Luckily Ted had not poured the tea. JP pitched right to avoid the cooker but bounced off the fridge, ricocheted against the ceiling and crashed in a heap onto the upended table just as Clare and Suzie arrived back from the shop with milk and fresh scones.

Ted set the pot of tea on the counter. Seeing stars, JP raked the air in front of him with his arms. Ted plucked a ragged sheet of paper from his son's dazed grasp.

'What's this?' Ted said.

'A measure trap,' JP said.

'A what?'

'He means "treasure map",' Suzie said. 'When he gets excited his sounds get mixed up. Remember that day at mass when he said, "Our Lord is a shoving leopard"?'

'Ah,' said Ted, unfolding the worn sheet and studying its squiggles. 'Right you are, JP. It *is* a treasure map. Where did you find it?'

'On prop of the tess.'

Clare chased Pucker, who was gobbling up stray bits of brown bread, out of the caravan and then extended her hand. 'Ted. Let me have a look at that.'

'You don't believe me?' he said.

'Of course not. You thought the change machine in the pub was a slot machine.'

On their way from Dublin they had stopped for lunch in Urlingford. After they had finished eating, while Clare was using the toilet, Ted had idly stuck a two-euro coin into the change machine. Coins rattled out. 'JP,' he had shouted after counting them, 'we broke even! What do you say we give it another go?'

'*You* thought that *I* thought it was a slot machine?' Ted now said. 'Hah! I didn't think you were so easily fooled, Clare. I was having a laugh with the children. You have to get up pretty late in the night to get one over on *me*.'

She didn't answer. Yesterday's black clouds still hung over her mood. She studied the map. 'This is ridiculous. It looks like something you'd find on the back of a cereal box. Or in a comic book.'

Ted peered over her shoulder. 'Clare, it's hand-drawn.'

'It's *printed*, Ted. It's only made to look like it's been drawn.'

'Mum, let me see.'

JP, Ted and Suzie huddled over the map.

'Look,' JP shouted, pointing at the drawing, 'that's our cove. It's the shame sape.'

'You know,' Suzie said, 'you're right. See how the rocks jut out?'

Ted pushed the head bandage from his eye. 'And if we just follow the dotted line ...' He pushed his finger along the treasure trail, lifting it from the map so that it pointed past the big fir tree by the car and into the tangle of gorse and old fencing on the hill beyond the laneway. 'Then the treasure will be ... just over that hill.'

'Can we go there, Dad?' JP shouted. 'Can we go there now? Please?'

JP was so excited he was starting to hover. Ted gently pressed him back to earth. 'Of course we can. Let's take those scones and head out.'

'Wait a minute,' Clare said. 'The kitchen is a disaster area. Who do you think is going to clean it up?'

'*Mum.*'

'Clare, there's time enough for the kitchen. We're on holiday.'

Clare huffed. 'A treasure map. That's ridiculous.'

'Ridiculous? I don't think so. There used to be pirates here. Isn't that right, kids? And where there are pirates, there must be –'

He grinned at JP.

'*Buried treasure!*' JP shouted.

'It's a wild goose chase, is what it is.'

'Please, Mum, *please.*'

Clare looked at Suzie, who usually backed her up. But even her eyes glittered with the prospect of gold doubloons and pieces of eight.

'All right, all right, go on. Find your hidden treasure. But I'm staying here. And Pucker stays with me. I need *some* company.'

'*Yaaay,*' they shouted (even Ted), as they ran across the laneway and disappeared into the gorse.

Clare took Pucker inside and closed the door. She gazed at the shambles in the kitchen, sighed and said to the dog, 'I don't know about you, Puck-a-luck, but I'm having a cup of tea before facing this mess.'

But Pucker was whining and scratching at the front door.

'Oh, no, you don't. You're staying in here with me, little doggie.'

She poured herself a cup of tea and sipped it while staring out the caravan window at the windy bay, flecked with whitecaps and sailing boats. The sky was beautiful today, a big blue dome, criss-crossed by seabirds and glittering with ocean spray. Ted was right, the kitchen could wait. And she had to admit, it was nice to have him and the kids out of her hair for a while. Sometimes it got so hectic she couldn't hear herself think.

But Pucker gave her no peace, scrabbling at the front door and threatening to rip its flimsy bottom rail to shreds. So let him follow the others, she thought, what was the harm? She opened the door and out he sprinted, but instead of heading after the kids he ran to a corner of the garden and started rooting in a patch of hummocky earth. Yapping and snorting, tail twitching, he burrowed furiously, clods of dirt flying between his legs.

'Pucker, what are you doing? Stop that! You're going to get filthy.'

But he was nosing and scrambling like a fox after a rabbit, and in a few minutes the hole was so deep only his hind legs were visible. Then an excited howl and the sound of his claws on wood. Clare peered in the hole and saw the corner of a box. Whining like a racing car, Pucker jumped in and out of the hole, his tongue hanging out. She got a spoon from the kitchen and dug around the chest until it was unearthed and she could lift it out of the hole.

'Well, Pucker, what have we here?'

The box was wooden but reinforced with metal edging. The lid was secured with an old-fashioned padlock. On top was a strange symbol made of two crossed sabres burned into the wood. Clare jiggled the lock and shook the box. Something inside clinked. Pucker bayed, head thrown back. Maybe JP *had* found a treasure map. Maybe it should have led to here, this strongbox, right under their noses. Ha! Wouldn't that show them! The rest of the family off running through the hills while *she* found the gold.

Pucker was whining and slobbering and butting the box with his head. Clare found a tyre iron in the boot of the car and used it to prise at the lid and batter the padlock, but the box was sealed tight as a bank safe. After ten minutes of fruitless effort, she laid the iron on the ground and stood up, breathing heavily.

Then she had an idea.

She checked up and down the coast. No one was in sight. She listened carefully for sounds of Ted and the kids. By now they were far away.

'Can you keep a secret, Pucker? Can you?'

One solid bolt of lightning and that locked box would spill its contents like a broken egg. She had told them all no powers on this holiday, but who was to know?

She fastened Pucker to his lead and led him to the caravan. They stood in the doorway while Clare concentrated. At once the sky filled with dark clouds. Heavy rumbling. She held her palms to her temples and stared hard at the treasure chest. Concentrated. Stared. Focused.

Sheets of rain, high winds – and *boom*! With a mighty roar and a brilliant flash, a spear of lightning zigzagged from the black clouds, directly towards – *oh, no* – the big pine tree. An explosion. Licks of fire around the trunk. The sound of wood straining and cracking, cracking and straining. As Clare stared in confusion the tree swayed and tottered and, with a ferocious whoosh, fell on top of the Fiasco, crushing its roof as if it were a matchbox.

The skies cleared at once. The air returned to perfect silence. Clare looked at Pucker. He barked.

With a small clink, the lock on the chest broke and the lid popped open.

Inside were old empty tins of dog food. Pucker nosed at them for a moment or two and then lay with his head between his paws as if nothing had happened.

6

Dazed
and
Confused

The Fiasco was a write-off. In fact, it was a fiasco.
The man from Baltimore Garage examined the
crushed car, barely visible beneath the bushy
branches of the broken tree. He took a long drag
from his cigarette and shook his shaved head.

'And you want me to do what?' he said.

The base of the tree was still smouldering. It was all Ted could do not to burst into flames himself. 'Tow it,' he said. 'Fix it.'

'It's not a tow truck you need, big fella, it's a chainsaw. Contact the forest service. That motor's banjaxed.'

'But I've had that car for ten years.'

'Is that a fact?'

Suzie and JP lingered behind their dad, fascinated by the spectacle and half hopeful, half fearful that he would blow his top. Clare was nowhere to be seen.

'Now what am I going to do?' Ted moaned.

The man grinned and blew smoke rings that expanded slowly in the still air. In his ear was a gold stud, on his arm a tattoo of a skull.

'That lad's a pirate,' JP whispered to Suzie.

'Shhh.'

'No worries,' the man said. 'You can hire a car from me.'

'A Fiasco?'

'Fresh out of Fiascos, I'm sorry to say, but I have a nippy little Opel Loco that would do you nicely. Or a super-charged Fireball if you don't mind spending a few squid.'

'No fireballs. Please.'

'The Loco, so.'

Ted tugged at his collar and his own smoke ring escaped. 'I'll get back to you,' he said.

The day was hot, the seaside dazzly with sunshine. The family walked along the coast road, on their way to the pirate museum, which had turned out to be a mile south of the village.

'I really don't understand why we have to walk,' Clare said. 'Suzie said that man offered you a perfectly good Loco at a decent price.'

'A Loco? Are you mental?'

'Dad,' JP said, 'why don't we wear superhero costumes?'

'You wear a cape.'

'Pucker, leave that dead bird alone!'

'I mean proper costumes, like Superman's – with bright colours and leggings and a big P on our chests.'

Suzie scanned the sky. Not a wisp of cloud. Not a hint of wind. The sea looked cool and inviting. A breeze off the water would be so soothing.

'Think about it, JP,' Clare said. 'If we wore costumes, Pucker would go ballistic. He would think they were uniforms.' She turned to Ted. 'And what's wrong with a Loco?'

JP said, 'But all other superheroes have costumes.'

'Why can't we go swimming?' Suzie whined. 'It's a gorgeous day and we have to be inside a museum.'

'Pirates, Suzie.'

'A Loco is tiny,' Ted said. 'The size of a fridge. If you think the four of us would fit into one of those, you're mad as a scientist.'

'Well, why not a different model?'

'He only had a Fireball.'

Clare smiled wearily. 'Why not? You and a Fireball would get on like a house on fire.'

Creating a bit of wind, Suzie thought, wouldn't be that different from weather resistance. Just concentrate in reverse.

Ted stopped on the roadway. 'Clare, if you hadn't smashed the Fiasco, then we'd still have a car. A perfectly good car.'

'Me? I smashed it?'

'Oh, so that was just a freak thunderstorm, I suppose.'

Suzie was roasting. She concentrated. All she wanted was a bit of air.

'Who was it that parked the car under that tree?' Clare said. 'Answer me that.'

Suzie felt a pop behind her eyes and a small but fierce tornado sprang up on the road in front of them. They all froze, except for Pucker. The dead bird in his mouth, he wandered into the cyclone and was lifted into its vortex, whirling in front of them as if in a food mixer. Fur and feathers. Squawks and doggie whimpers.

'Clare,' Ted shouted, 'what are you doing? No weather power!'

'It's not me!'

Suzie stopped concentrating. Like magic, the tornado disappeared, leaving Pucker suspended in mid-air for a split second before he fell to the tarmac with a thud. The bird, alive after all, flapped away.

'Poor Pucker,' Ted said, as he and Clare crouched to look after him. 'Are you OK, pooch? Are you all right Pucker-stucker?'

Pucker blinked and bobbed and barely barked.

JP stood in the road and stamped his foot. 'You're all ignoring me. I want a costume. With a pig bee on my chest.'

'Poor little Puckster.'

'He wants a costume,' Suzie mocked. 'With a pig bee.'

'It's not fair,' he shouted. 'I believe I can fly. I believe I can touch the sky. I'm a superhero.'

'Good for you.'

'I'm pooper-soured.'

Clare stood up, hands on her hips. 'All right, JP, that's quite enough of that language.'

Pucker raised himself from the road and shook his head and shoulders. His collar jangled.

'Arf,' he said.

7

Ship
of
Fools

The museum doors were locked.

'What time is it?'

'Eleven.'

'It's closed.'

'The man said they were open today. Nine to six.'

'We trudged all the way out here,' Clare said, 'and it's *closed*?'

'Let's go swimming,' Suzie said.

Ted cupped his hands around his eyes and peered through the glass door. 'Oh, wow!'

'What, Dad, *what*?'

'JP, have a look. Pirates, all right.'

In the darkened depths of the museum, JP could make out shadowy figures in long coats and tricorn hats, the glint of cutlasses and daggers, tattered flags hanging from beams, a weathered wooden chest spilling gold coins, a cannon and thick coils of rope.

'Dad, we have to get in there, we *have* to.'

Breathing hard, Mr Beasley shuffled into view from around the side of the building. The day before, on the pier, he had been elegant and smartly dressed. Today he was rumpled and unshaven. He wore a woollen greatcoat decorated with dirty gold braid, baggy pantaloons and a red bandana. Tucked into his belt were a pair of silver-painted plastic swords, the kind that children wave at birthday parties. Pucker growled.

'Terribly sorry,' Mr Beasley said. 'You caught us on our elevenses.'

He patted his pockets, looking for keys. Sweat dripped from his face like tears.

'*Fitzhugh,*' he brayed, before turning to Ted and Clare and bowing. 'Let me introduce myself. Edwin Beasley, proprietor of Baltimore's World-Famous Museum of Pirates and Buccaneers. You are very welcome. *Fitzhugh!*'

Fitzhugh appeared from the other side of the building, wiping his lips with his sleeve. His eyebrows twitched wildly and his beard was dotted with biscuit crumbs. 'Yes, Mr Beasley.'

'The key, man, give me the key.'

'I don't have it, Mr Beasley.'

'Of course you do, you idiot, you locked up not ten minutes ago.'

Wincing as if he thought he was about to be hit, Fitzhugh pointed a trembling finger at a strand of yellow yarn poking from the breast pocket of Mr Beasley's greatcoat. Eyes rolling, Mr Beasley yanked the key from his pocket, unlocked the door and ushered the family into the museum. Dogs were not allowed, so Fitzhugh was told to tie Pucker's lead to a fence post and bring him a bowl of fresh water.

Inside it was dark and cool. The museum was done up like a ship, with a pinewood deck and raised steering platform, oak masts and drooping canvas sails. Dummies dressed like pirates swabbed the deck and climbed the rigging. A few sat beside the cannon, cleaning their pistols and muskets. The open chest overflowed with pieces of eight. Beside it stood the captain, staring at the horizon with a telescope. He had a wooden leg, and on his shoulder was a tiny monkey with sharp yellow teeth and a beady-eyed stare.

'Dad, look at me!'

'Leave the ropes where they are, JP.'

'Quite all right,' Mr Beasley said, wiping his brow with the bandana. 'Let the lad explore. We're very interactive here. And historically accurate. Everything in the museum is based on the famous pirate raid of 1631. Right here in Baltimore.'

'There were pirates here?' Ted asked.

'There most certainly were. The meanest, nastiest, bloodthirstiest Barbary pirates ever to sail the North Atlantic. From Algiers they were.' Mr Beasley had calmed down. His voice bounced around the high-ceilinged room like a teacher's. 'This fearsome gang of cut-throats terrorised the Irish sea lanes for many a year. They were led by the notorious Jan Jansen, a Dutchman also known as Morat Rais. His speciality was capturing white slaves and bringing them back to North Africa. He was wild looking, with a long grey beard and manic eyes.'

'*Aaaaaaahhh*,' Suzie screamed. 'There he is! He's *alive*.'

Sure enough, a bearded pirate had come to life behind one of the ship's portholes, grimacing and pointing at JP, who was climbing the rigging. Terrified, JP slipped and fell. He saved himself by going into fly mode at the last second and landing delicately on the deck. Suzie kept screaming. Ted pulled a sabre from the dummy captain's belt and jumped in front of his children. The captain rocked back and forth until he tipped over and hit the deck so hard his head fell off and the little monkey bounced off his shoulder and across the pine boards as if alive, rolling to a stop between Clare's feet, so that *she* started screaming too.

'It's all right,' Mr Beasley shouted. 'Nothing to fear!'

The porthole was a window overlooking the yard. The bearded pirate was Fitzhugh.

'You moron,' Mr Beasley yelled at him, waving his own tiny sword, 'go and look after the dog!'

Clare kicked the monkey so that it flew across the deck and lodged in the mouth of the cannon. Ted tried to reinsert the captain's head, but his hand slipped and tore the captain's wig off.

'Just leave things *as they are*,' Mr Beasley said, a little too testily. 'We'll fix it later.'

After a few minutes everyone calmed down, though the pirate ship looked as if it had been attacked. Mr Beasley lifted his hand dramatically. 'Perhaps this is all too much for you,' he said. 'Perhaps it's not a good idea to go below deck, to where the *real* terrors lie.'

He let his hand drop and pointed at the floor.

'No, we want to go,' JP shouted. 'We *want* to.'

'Show us your worst,' Ted said. 'We've seen a few terrors in our day.'

Mr Beasley led them down several flights of wooden steps to the lowest deck of the ship. The deeper they went, the darker and damper it became. When they reached the bottom, he stopped them with an outstretched hand. 'This is where they stored the cables,' he whispered, 'and the *slaves*.'

JP had imagined African men in chains, but when his eyes adjusted to the gloomy room, the dummies he saw manacled to the low beams of the stuffy bunker were Europeans, mostly women and children.

'Janey mackers,' Suzie said.

'This didn't *really* happen,' Clare said.

'It most assuredly did, madam. It was the night of the twentieth of June, the shortest night of the year. The year 1631. A full moon cast a blue light on Baltimore Harbour. Two hours before dawn Captain Rais piloted his ships into the very bay

you can see through that window. He lowered anchor and sent two hundred North African pirates ashore, under the cover of darkness. These bloodthirsty men ransacked the village, killed without mercy those who resisted and took a hundred and seven prisoners back to the ships: men, women and children, families just like yourselves. As you see, they were bound in chains in this foul-smelling room and were eventually brought to the Barbary coast.'

Mr Beasley went silent. Faintly, far above, they could hear Pucker barking.

'What happened to them when they got there?' Suzie said, pointing at a girl of her own age who lay face down on the floor, her hands bound together.

'They became the slaves of the Ottoman Grand Pasha of Algiers. Children were separated from their parents. Women became house servants to the sultans. And the men ...' Mr Beasley looked at Ted. 'The strong fishing men of Baltimore became galley slaves on the pirate ships, chained day and night to the oars and literally *worked to death*.'

They stared for a long, quiet minute at the dummies.

'The savages,' Ted said.

'Those people never saw their homes again.'

Ted was beginning to crackle and spark. Clare

suggested they go back upstairs. On deck, a light breeze wafted through open windows.

But Ted was still heating up. 'Clare, we have to do something about this.'

'It happened nearly four hundred years ago, Ted.'

'Such injustice! Didn't we swear to –'

'Cool down.'

'Pirate raids, right here in this village. Innocent families.'

'But that's not the end of the story,' Mr Beasley said softly.

'No?'

'No. Down through the centuries, to this very day, the descendants of those evil men have vowed to return to Baltimore and repeat their horrible deed.'

'I'd like to see them try it,' Ted said.

'On every anniversary of the raid, the night of the twentieth of June, the villagers light a bonfire on the beach and guard the bay.'

'The twentieth?' Clare said. 'Sure, that's this weekend.'

'It is indeed, madam. And you would all be doing us a great service if you kept careful watch yourselves.'

'Of course we will,' Ted said.

Mr Beasley lifted the telescope from the headless captain's grasp and handed it to JP. 'A souvenir for the young lad, and something to help you keep a lookout.'

'*Thanks.*'

'Don't mention it. You can't be too careful. And you have no idea how much your vigilance might help us.'

As the Powers headed down the winding road towards the village, Mr Beasley and Fitzhugh watched them through the museum's front window.

'Do you think they'll bite, Mr Beasley?'

'*Bite?* They'll swallow it whole, Fitzhugh. Hook, line and sinker. Once that tall ship comes down from Galway for the weekend, they'll be on it like wasps on a jam jar. Wreaking havoc.'

'I don't know. That young one seems a dark horse.'

'*Hah.* She's a fool. Like the rest of them. Remember when we robbed the *Book of Smells* from St Malodourous College and the Powers got on the case? The famous *Powers.* They caused a thunderstorm *inside* the college library and soaked all those rare books. And that stupid little boy flew through a precious stained-glass window. Caused such a ruckus we got away *no* problem. Well, it will be the same this time around.'

'If you say so, sir.'

'Once they go after the tall ship, every man and woman in the Garda, navy and coast guard will be busy dealing with the chaos. We'll sail out of here like a couple of fishermen.'

'Genius, sir.'

'Is the boat fully loaded?'

'It is.'

'All treasure on board?'

'Every piece.'

'Excellent. We'll be rich, Fitzhugh, filthy rich. The *Book of Smells*. The Gangrene Gargoyle. The Cross of Ballyuseless. All worth millions. And after we meet our Russian friends in Montenegro we can retire to a tropical island and never have to work again. Think of what your five per cent will buy you.'

'I thought you said ten per cent.'

'Don't be greedy, Fitzhugh. You couldn't possibly spend five per cent of what we'll be making. Not in the whole of the rest of your sad, miserable little life.'

'What about the museum, sir?'

'The museum? Let the town take it over. See if they can earn back that pathetic grant they gave us. Maybe they can give tours to the local yokels and finish by telling them the story of the dastardly Edwin Beasley, *the greatest pirate of them all.*'

His evil laugh filled the museum. His gold tooth glinted. Far ahead, Suzie, walking at the rear of the family's single file, glanced back at them over her shoulder.

8

After
Midnight

The caravan was long and thin, like a railway carriage, with the kitchen and sitting-room in the centre, a master bedroom to the right, and two bedrooms on the left-hand side, overlooking the sea. Suzie and JP each had one of these tiny rooms, not much wider than a single bed and with small hinged windows looking out on the cove.

The night after the visit to the pirate museum, Suzie lay in her bed reading. Outside her window, a full moon hung over Sherkin Island, and a silver path of reflected moonlight led from the edge of the cove to the island shore. As she read she soon became aware of a steady thudding, as if someone outside was, over and over, lifting a stone and letting it drop to the ground. She opened the window and listened carefully. The sound was close but muffled. And it was familiar. She concentrated. She could have turned on her sonic hearing if she'd wanted to, but sometimes that hurt her ears. Besides, this was a sound she *knew*. From home.

Ah. Of course. JP was practising his flying. In his room.

But his bedroom light was off. When she turned it on she saw him hovering high above the bed in his Spiderman pyjamas, fast asleep. His head was bumping into the skylight, like a moth hitting a light bulb.

'Uh-oh,' she said.

She turned off the light and crept softly to her parents' bedroom.

'Dad,' she whispered. 'Mum.'

They were also asleep. She shook her mother's shoulder.

'Suzie? What is it?'

Ted stirred. 'What's going on?'

'It's JP,' Suzie said. 'He's doing it again. Sleep-flying.'

It happened when he was under stress. The night before a school test. When he acted in the school play. When Pucker got sick. Sleep-flying. The covers would fall off him and he would rise towards the ceiling like a hot-air balloon. One summer night he had drifted through his open window and sleep-flown as far as Dublin Airport, throwing air-traffic control into chaos and delaying all arrivals for hours. Since then his parents kept the window shut. And another thing about JP's sleep-flying: you couldn't just wake him up and tell him to go back to bed. Because as soon as he was awake and his brain returned to normal mode, he'd fall to the floor like a bag of sugar.

'Get the pillows,' Clare whispered.

Ted and Suzie fetched pillows from all the beds as well as duvets, sofa cushions and Pucker's bean-bag bed. They piled them below JP, but as soon as they were perfectly set up for a soft landing he drifted to the left, so they had to move them carefully to the other side of the room.

They waited to see if he would stay where he was. His head bumped against the corner where the wall met the ceiling, but he did not drift.

'OK,' Clare said, 'are you ready?'

'Go ahead,' Ted said.

Gently she reached up and tapped JP's shoulder. His eyes fluttered open.

'Mum, what are you doing standing down there?' He yawned, still afloat, and then went bug-eyed with fright. 'And what am I doing *highing up leer*?'

He flapped his hands like a duck, just enough to propel himself beyond the safety zone of the cushions, and then plummeted to the hard floor with a nasty splat.

'JP,' Ted said, 'how many times have I told you – don't flap when you wake up.'

JP was waving away the stars that orbited his dazed head.

'Dad,' Suzie said, 'I don't think this is a good time for a lecture.'

'Nuckabeers,' JP said, pointing at the window. His telescope leaned against the sill. 'I saw them. Nuckabeers on a bold note.'

Clare helped JP up from the floor and hugged him. 'There, there, pet. You had a bad dream. All that talk about pirates today got you excited, and you flew in your sleep and had a nightmare about buccaneers.'

She smiled at Ted over JP's shoulder.

'No,' JP said. 'Really. Tell them, Suzie.'

'You had a bad dream, JP.'

Ted picked up the pillows. 'OK, everyone, back to sleep. It's after midnight.'

Clare tucked JP into bed.

'Nuckabeers,' he said dreamily.

She shook her head and said to Ted, 'I told you that museum was a bad idea.'

An hour later Suzie was in her own deep snooze, dreaming of Peter Pan, when the overhead light woke her. JP stood at the end of her bed. She squinted at him. His mouth was slack, his face the colour of low-fat milk.

'What's wrong?' she said.

'I saw ... I saw ... I saw ...'

'What?'

'In my skeletope.'

'Calm down, JP.'

'In my skeletope I saw a ...'

'What did you see?'

'A teleskin.'

'Teleskin?'

'Suzie. I saw a teleskin in my skeletope.'

Her eyes grew large as plums. She hissed, 'You saw a *skeleton* in your *telescope*?'

'Yes!'

She let her head drop to the pillow. Looking up at the ceiling, she said, 'JP, you really have to control your imagination. You're only scaring yourself.'

JP pointed at the window. 'Look, Suzie. Look out there.'

The way he spoke was so weird that Suzie knelt on the bed and looked out. Sure enough, floating near the island, silhouetted in moonlight, was an old wooden ship, with three masts, square sails and rigging like a giant spider's web.

'Get your telescope,' she told him.

JP was back in seconds. Her heart galloping, Suzie took a look. At first she saw nothing but moonlit water and dark clouds, but suddenly the side of the ship appeared in the telescope's magnified circle. Slowly she panned upward and saw the ship's dark hull, the gaping gunports and the deck. Another inch and there was the skeleton, bound to the rigging with its arms spread and its skull grinning.

She screamed. And screamed and screamed. Ted and Clare ran into the room. Ted's hair was sticking straight up, as if *he* was the one who was terrified.

'*Now* what?' he said.

'Pirates,' Suzie shouted.

'Ah, for the love of –'

Suzie pointed at the window. 'Out there!'

Ted peered out. 'I don't see anything.'

'The ship, Dad, the ship.'

'That's Sherkin Island, Suzie.'

She went to the window. The dark blob of the island. The magic carpet of moonlight. The blue-black water. But no ship.

'It was there a minute ago.'

But now she doubted her own eyes. JP was so wired he had *her* seeing things too.

Ted rubbed his chin with his hand. He picked up the book Suzie had been reading. *Treasure Island*. He put on his no-more-messing face. 'Kids,' he said, 'can I get a *little* bit of sleep tonight? Please?'

JP was hopping from foot to foot. 'We saw it, Mum, we saw it. A teleskin.'

'Really, Suzie,' Clare said. 'We expect a bit more common sense from you.'

'But I ... I really thought that ...'

Clare put her arms around both children. 'We're on holiday. We're here to relax. So let's forget about the pirate museum and white slavery and those other horrible things Mr Beasley told us about. They happened hundreds and hundreds of years ago. Let's all get a good sleep. In the morning we can go for an early swim and I'll make pancakes for breakfast.'

For the next hour, Suzie was up and down from her bed, checking the bay. Nothing. She decided that she had been seeing things and eventually fell asleep. But not JP. In his room he stayed glued to the window, telescope at the ready, elbows perched on the sill, waiting for the pirates to return. *He* wasn't going to let down his guard. *He* wasn't going to let the family be kidnapped. He even crept to the living-room and got their mum's camera. He would show them. Imagination? *Hah*. With Pucker beside him, he kept vigil throughout the night, ready to raise the alarm and save the day.

But the ship did not reappear, and when morning arrived Clare found him curled on the floor beneath the window, his face pale, his hair mussed, Pucker's head nestled in the crook of his arm like a teddy bear.

9

He Ain't
Heavy,
He's My
Brother

In the morning JP and Ted walked down to the village to buy a newspaper. Nothing was out of the ordinary: boats on the water, fishermen in the harbour, holidaymakers lining up to take the ferry to the island.

'Does this look like a town that's been attacked by pirates?' Ted asked.

'Maybe they're waiting for the right time. When nobody suspects.'

'Lulling us into a false sense of security?' Ted said. 'Not a bad theory, JP. But why didn't they make their move last night so? Everyone asleep. Nobody expecting them. It's like I always say: you can lead a ship to water, but you can't make it sink.'

'What does that mean?'

'What it means is, we'll cross that bridge when the well runs dry.'

As usual, his dad was too clever for him. And JP was not in great form. All around him were children on holiday, laughing and playing in the sunshine. Yet he felt only doom. He couldn't forget the image of the grinning skeleton. In his head it was saying, 'I'm going to get you!' And this whole harbour scene felt wrong, like the moment in the movie when everything looks happy and normal until the camera pulls back and reveals the wicked witch watching everything in her crystal ball and cackling before she sends the evil monkeys flapping into the purple sky.

He needed to do something. Back at the caravan he fetched the treasure map from under his mattress and showed it to Suzie.

'Look at these coves,' he said, running his finger over the map. 'Perfect hiding places for pirates. For pirate ships.'

'Not that map again – you know, JP, when we go back to school you should bring it to geography class.'

'I'm serious – if we follow the coastline, we'll find the pirates. I know it.'

'Like we found buried treasure?'

'We have to find that ship, Suzie. Who knows *what* they're planning. And that skeleton!'

Suzie shuddered and closed her eyes. But she said, 'There is no ship, JP.'

'But you saw it!'

'I don't know what I saw.'

'Well, if you don't come, I'll go by myself. Me and Pucker. And I don't care if I have to walk all day. I'll find it, I'm telling you!'

He thrust out his jaw and clenched his fists. His hair stuck up in the back in springy tufts. He didn't know it, but Suzie found him comical when he was angry.

'Oh, don't be a pain,' she said, trying not to laugh. 'I'll come with you.'

Ted and Clare were playing cards on the patio. Suzie told them they were going exploring.

'Where?' Clare asked.

'Just along the beach.'

'Be careful – and be back in an hour. We're going to play pitch and putt.'

'Can you believe it?' JP muttered as they left the caravan. 'We could be kidnapped tonight and be carried off in chains to China, and Mum and Dad want to play *pitch and putt!*'

Beyond the caravan, the sea path followed the beach for a few hundred metres. Then it went up along a ridge covered in gorse, which had a steep drop to the strand on one side. Pucker led the way, darting into the scrub every now and then to roust a seabird or wrestle with a stick. Suzie stayed to the rear, watching her brother and the dog carefully. The further they walked, the higher they rose, until the rocky beach was so far beneath them that the roar of surf was as distant as the sound of a conch shell held to your ear. And there was no wall or fence beside the path – they were walking along the edge of a cliff that was getting higher and higher.

They reached a peak where they could see the coast ahead for half a mile or so – a long stretch of empty strand.

'Look,' Suzie said, 'there's no ship. There's no anything. Let's go back.'

'It could be over there,' JP said, pointing. 'Behind that headland.'

'Oh, *headland*. Aren't we the little geographer.'

'It's behind there, Suzie. I can feel it, I tell you.'

He was already moving up the path again. A boy on a mission.

'Just be careful,' she said. 'And watch Pucker. He's running too close to the edge.'

But JP was well ahead of her, with Pucker barking in his wake. And was Suzie imagining it, or were there distant clanking and shuffling sounds and a roll of deep voices singing a sea shanty?

'Slow down,' she shouted.

She ran after JP and Pucker, breathing heavily. After a while, they trotted around a bend in the path. But by the time Suzie reached the bend, they had disappeared, even though there was at least a hundred metres of empty pathway in front of her. Where could they be? They hadn't been running *that* fast.

'JP, where are you? Pucker? Here, boy. Here, Pucker-stuck.'

She walked briskly. No sign of them. In the distance she saw – was that Mr Beasley? Staring at her with binoculars from the top of the headland?

She broke into a run. She stopped. 'JP. JP!'

Now she was really scared.

A sudden blur from the bushes. A glint of steel.

'*En garde!*'

JP leapt from the gorse, waving an old piece of pipe like a sword. Screaming in fright, Suzie ducked out of the way, tripped on a tree root and fell hard to the ground, twisting her ankle. At the same time, Pucker, revved into a frenzy by the commotion, came barrelling out of the gorse, ran through JP's legs, tumbled over Suzie's feet and somersaulted – *over the cliff.*

The whole world went still. No wind, no sea, no bird calls. Time stopped. JP dropped his sword and stared at the empty patch of sky that had swallowed Pucker. He was paralysed. He couldn't speak. Total silence.

Something snapped in his head and the world returned to life.

Suzie was yelling at him. 'I'm hurt. *I can't get up!'*

JP rushed around her and peered over the cliff edge. Three metres below was Pucker. His frightened face stared up at JP and his front paws clung to a narrow ledge of stone. The rest of his body dangled above the precipice – thirty metres at least to jagged rocks below.

'Pucker,' JP said in a terrified whisper, 'don't move.'

'What's going on?' Suzie shouted from the path.

JP turned around. He was crying. 'It's Pucker,' he said. 'The lore dittle poggie's *fanging* by his *heat*.'

Suzie's couldn't move her foot without a jagged electric pain shooting up her leg. She gritted her teeth and said, 'JP – calm down. Listen to me. We can work this out. Come over here and help me up.'

But JP wasn't listening. His eyes had glazed over and his face had the look he got when he was about to do something foolish. He backed away from the cliff. Assumed his take-off position.

'No,' Suzie shouted. 'Don't do it, JP. You're out of practice!'

But he was rocking back and forth, getting ready for the leap.

Suzie focused on her mother. She had sent her mum mind messages before, but never at such a distance. *Come now. Please come now. Along the sea path. It's an emergency.* She put all her energy into the message. Her head pounded in time with her sore ankle.

With a yell JP sprinted towards the cliff and flew into the void. Suzie heard him zip away. Pucker whimpered. Desperate, she dragged herself to the edge and looked down. Pucker's tail wagged when he saw her. He was hanging onto

the ledge by his claws. In the vast curve of earth above the bay, JP's tiny form was shooting back and forth like a Hallowe'en rocket, with no sense of direction or control. And no sign of her mother. Suzie clutched her face in her hands.

What should she do? What *could* she do? A whirlwind that might lift Pucker from the ledge and blow him to safety? No – look what had happened when she'd tried to create a breeze on the way to the museum. Fire? Ridiculous. How about telekinesis? But that only worked for sliding or shuffling or redirecting. How could it move a fifteen-kilo dog up and over a *cliff*?

More whimpers. The scrape of canine nails on granite. Pucker was losing his grip! He was about to fall to a gruesome doggie death!

Off in the wild blue yonder, JP gradually got control of his flight and guided himself back towards Pucker. From a great height he swooped low across water and strand, speeding towards the rocks at the base of the cliff. *I'm going to do it*, he said to himself as the wind whistled past his ears. *I'm going to save Pucker*. Two seconds later the cliff-face loomed in front of him. To avoid crashing into the rocks he had to pull back at the last moment so that he was flying straight up, inches from the granite, directly towards Pucker's hanging body and Suzie's frightened face peering over the cliff.

Pucker barked desperately. His nails scraped and scrabbled. His paws gave way – and he fell.

Suzie screamed. But Pucker going down hit JP coming up, landing on the boy's head and slowing him down. With the terrified dog wrapped around his face, JP gradually came to a stop in mid-air, like a kite in a dying wind, just feet from where Suzie lay. She reached for the scruff of Pucker's neck, but it was inches beyond her fingertips. Sapped of energy, JP fell earthwards, but his belt looped over a protruding rock and there he dangled, with Pucker hanging on for dear life.

Suzie looked down at the writhing mass of fur and tracksuit. If JP couldn't see, he would lose his flying power. Pucker and JP, her closest friends in the world, were a thin, straining leather belt away from plunging to their deaths!

Without thinking, without even having to concentrate, she felt her powers take over. She could do it, she could! Hadn't she redirected cars going at a hundred and twenty kilometres an hour? Created a tornado that lifted Pucker high in the air? With a huge whoosh she moved a fierce wind off the sea, which followed the same path as JP had and lifted him and Pucker into the air, catapulted them back over the cliff edge and spilled them on to the path.

They lay there, dazed.

JP pushed Pucker from his face. 'What happened?' he said.

Suzie lay propped on her elbows, her foot pounding with pain. Seeing JP and Pucker safe made her want to cry. 'You did it, JP. You saved Pucker. You flew down there and saved him.'

JP shook his head in amazement. 'Suzie, you wouldn't believe it. I've never flown so well. It was easy. Like I was being lifted through the air by another superhero!'

'Wow!'

As she spoke, Ted and Clare came running around the bend.

'Suzie,' Clare shouted, 'what happened?'

'Dad,' JP yelled, 'I saved Pucker! He fell off the cliff and I *saved* him!'

'I had the most terrible dream,' Clare said.

'She ran out of the house,' Ted said. 'Like a bull in a chip shop. I could barely keep up with her.'

'Mum, you came.'

'A mother's intuition is never wrong.'

Clare helped Suzie.

JP told the story.

Ted grew stern.

'What did I tell you two about these ridiculous claims? A pirate ship? Really. And then you go on this – what does your mother call it? – wild gooseberry chase. And look what happens. Someone could get seriously injured. Suzie *is* injured.'

He stood with his back to the sea. The kids had gone totally quiet. Slack-mouthed. Saucer-eyed. For once they were listening to him without interrupting. Finally, he was getting some respect. The attention a father deserved.

'All this nonsense about pirates,' he said. '*Ships*. As if here, in this sleepy town ...'

Wait a minute. That wasn't respect on the children's faces. Or on Clare's. It was ... *fear*.

Speechless, they pointed. He turned around.

Out on the waves, emerging from behind the headland, was a huge three-masted sailing ship, with bandana-headed pirates stalking the deck and waving their swords, a red-coated captain staring at the cove through a telescope and a skull-and-crossbones flag fluttering from the mainmast.

10

Won't
Get
Fooled
Again

Ted loved family meetings. The television shows he'd watched as a boy always had them: *Little House on the Prairie, Dallas, The Waltons.* When the wolves howled in prairie darkness and the men in black hats saddled up their horses, nothing was more important than a family meeting. The power of evil must be met by the power of love.

They gathered in the sitting-room of the caravan, Ted, Clare and JP at the tiny chrome dining table, Suzie stretched out on the sofa, her bandaged ankle resting on a pillow, her crutches leaning against the wall.

'Are you all right, pet?' Clare asked.

'I'm fine, Mum.'

After Suzie had fallen Ted had carried her back to the caravan. He and Clare worried that her ankle was broken but had no car to bring her to the hospital in.

JP had suggested that they contact Superman.

'Mum, he has X-ray vision. All he has to do is look at Suzie's foot and he'll see if anything is broken.'

'Don't be ridiculous. He lives in America.'

'He could fly here in, like, five seconds,' JP said.

It had always been his dream to meet Superman.

'We're not calling Superman,' Ted said sternly. He said to Clare, 'He's on the association committee. Who expelled us.'

'*Super*man,' Clare said, shaking her head. 'Man of *Steel*. He thinks he's so cool.'

Finally they called a taxi, which took Suzie to the clinic. Nothing was broken, but she had sprained it badly, and the doctor gave her crutches and told her to stay off the foot. Ted and

Clare were relieved, but the matter of the pirate ship was a bigger concern.

To start the family meeting Ted said, 'We need a plan.'

This was the way he began every meeting. With a deep voice. And a finger in the air.

'What we need, Ted,' Clare said, 'is to use our powers.'

Ted nodded gravely. 'I know. The holiday is officially over. Did you see those pirates? The looks on their faces? They're going to make their move tonight, you can be sure of that.'

'Why don't I whip up a storm,' Clare said, 'and drive them back out to sea?'

'I thought of that. But wouldn't they just sail back the next day?'

'Unless the ship sank.'

'Mum,' Suzie said, 'you'll drown them. They may be pirates, but they're also human beings.'

Ted and Clare looked at Suzie as if they had forgotten she was there. Of course, she didn't have any powers.

'I'm sure they have lifeboats,' Clare said.

'The *Titanic* had lifeboats.'

'We're not dealing with ordinary people,' Ted said. 'Remember what Mr Beasley told us – these cut-throats are the descendants of the original pirates of 1631. Bloodthirsty brigands who kidnapped over a hundred villagers and sold them into slavery. And they have made a solemn vow to repeat their horrible deed.'

'But that doesn't mean –'

Suzie stopped mid-sentence. Beasley. Suddenly she remembered how, just before she had fallen, she had seen him on the headland, peering at her through binoculars. What had he been doing up there? And if he'd seen her falling and hurting herself, then why hadn't he come down to help?

'It's such an exciting event,' Beasley was saying at that very moment, less than a mile from the Powers' caravan. 'It will be a night that the town of Baltimore will never forget.'

He stood on the deck of the *Rabid Buffoon* talking to its captain, a fat Frenchman with a pencil moustache, a bright red coat and a stuffed parrot loosely clipped to his shoulder.

'We are at your service, *monsieur*,' the captain said. He bowed as he spoke, so that the parrot swung from his shoulder and stabbed him in the chest. 'Mairzy doats,' he cried, yanking the beak from his flesh and resetting the bird. A dark spot of blood appeared on his tunic.

Alarmed, Beasley asked, 'Are you all right, sir?'

The captain waved away the question with a sneer. 'It is nothing. A mere peck.'

When the captain wasn't volunteering to help on the tall ship, he ran a bicycle repair shop in Bordeaux. Of course he didn't *do* anything on the ship – no actual piloting or captaining or ordering – but the ship's sponsors thought they needed a figurehead to stand on the deck, peer through a telescope and look captainly.

'We have some special effects set up for this evening,' Beasley said. 'Air, water and fire.'

'What do you mean?'

'Oh, you know: wind machines, fireworks, maybe even a hologram of Peter Pan flying through the sky.'

'*Très chic.*'

'And you should play your part. The cannon, the sword-waving. Get your men to put on their fiercest faces. We want the citizens of Baltimore to feel as if a *real* pirate ship is attacking them.'

'But of course.'

'The townspeople will be eternally in your debt. But if I may be so bold as to request one little thing? Please don't mention these arrangements to anyone. We want it to be, you know – a surprise.'

The captain touched a wing of his large red nose and stuck out his purple lower lip. 'You can count on me, *monsieur*.'

'I know,' JP shouted, jumping up from the table. He had said nothing during the meeting so far. 'Why don't I fly to the tops of the masts and untie the rigging? Then the sails will fall on top of the pirates and they'll get all tangled up and the ship can't move anyway because it has no sails and then I can grab a rope and fly around them so that they're all tied up and they can breathe through the sails, so it's not like they're in any real danger, and – '

'Quiet,' Ted shouted. 'JP, please. You're like a cat on a hot tin can. I can't hear myself blink.'

'Ted, he's just making a suggestion.'

'I know, Clare. But this isn't a game we're playing. The future of this town is at stake. Of the country. The nation depends on us. It always has.' He stood up from the table and put his hand to his heart. 'Who are we?'

'The Powers!' JP yelled.

'And what are we?'

'We're super.'

'Super what?'

'Super-powered!'

Suzie sighed.

Pucker barked.

Ted sat down again.

'Right,' he said. 'So here's what we're going to do.'

Fitzhugh led Beasley to the sheltered inlet. To anyone passing, the cove would appear like any other – nothing but ragged underbrush and random stones. But when Fitzhugh parted the dense growth of pine and lifted the camouflaging branches one by one, what was revealed was ... buried treasure?

Not quite. An old boat, worn and unpainted, with faded markings and a broken helm. It looked like a long-abandoned fishing craft that would barely stay afloat, let alone make its way across the stormy waves of the mid-Atlantic and the crowded Mediterranean to the golden shores of Montenegro.

But inside it was water-tight and fully seaworthy and crammed from bow to stern with high-tech navigational equipment, state-of-the-art weaponry, a month's worth of food and drink and the treasure: the precious national heirlooms the two men had painstakingly stolen from Irish museums and libraries over the last twelve months.

Beasley stroked his chin. His eyes glittered with greed. 'Excellent, Fitzhugh, excellent.'

'When is the attack, sir?'

'You leave that to me. I want you to stay right here, eyes peeled. As soon as you hear the Powers attack the tall ship, you launch the boat and flash your torch three times in the direction of the headland.'

'But why all this tall ship business, sir? Why don't we just leave in the middle of the night?'

'Did I tell you to think, Fitzhugh? What was our most successful robbery?'

'Malodorous College.'

'And why did we get away so easily?'

'Because of the Powers. The commotion they caused.'

'And who's a moron?'

'I am, sir.'

'Yes. So flash your torch when I tell you and I will join you and we shall be on our way to riches.'

'Brilliant, sir. Absolutely brilliant.'

'So,' Ted said, 'is that clear to everyone? JP?'

'I fly back and forth across the ship's bow, creating a distraction.'

'Clare?'

'I generate a tidal wave and direct the ship towards the coast-guard station.'

'A *gentle* tidal wave. Just enough to nudge it towards the shore. Then I'll throw a fireball or two onto the deck – small ones, but enough to disable the ship – while Suzie ... Suzie, what's your job?'

'What, Dad?'

'Suzie, concentrate! You watch from here with the telescope, and when the ship is disabled you ring the guards from my mobile phone. They'll contact the coast guard. You see, pet, just because you don't have powers doesn't mean that you don't have an important part to play.'

But Suzie didn't hear him. Outside, faint but clear to her sharpened hearing, was the lingering echo of a familiar evil laugh.

11

Riders on the Storm

'Dad.'

   'Inclination angle, forty-three degrees ...'

   '*Dad.*'

   '... fifty-seven kilometres an hour ...'

   'Dad, something came through the letter box!'

   Ted looked at Suzie. His face was fuzzy. He had lost track of time.

This always happened before a super job. Clare and JP were in their bedrooms, 'preparing'. Clare got ready for battle by thinking about the Greek gods of weather: Aeolus, Zeus and Poseidon. 'They were the original superheroes,' she claimed. 'They inspire me.' But what they really did was put her to sleep.

And JP? Well, he prepared by banging his head against the wall. As he put it, 'It feels so good when I stop.' He was definitely a boy with a problem.

But Ted liked to *plan*. Diagrams, timelines, schedules. Maps and scale drawings and cross sections. Graphs and charts.

So Suzie, stuck on the sofa with a sore foot and a bad temper, sulked and tried to get her dad to focus.

'Don't distract me, pet, I'm nearly there,' Ted muttered, spreading a sheet of poster paper on the table and stitching dotted lines around a badly drawn pirate ship. 'I've worked out JP's flying speed and inclination angle for maximum distraction potential. I've calculated the trajectory requirements of my fireballs. And I have found the precise equations for the definition pitch and frequency rate for your mother's tidal wave.' He pounded the floor with his wellingtons and threw his head back. '*Yabbablabbasuperblue!*' he screamed. 'The whole thing will be a perfect storm. When those fireballs hit the poop deck, the pirates won't know what hit them! The crew will run around, trying to put out the flames. Clare's waves will rock the boat, the pirates will slip and slide all over the shop, eh, I mean the *ship*, yes, the ship will come to a standstill. Chaos. Evil unmasked. Then you dial the mobile, and the coast guard comes to the rescue. The Powers save the day. Again. *Brilliant!*'

Suzie pointed at the slip of paper lying beneath the letter slot.

'Dad.'

'Quiet, Suzie, I'm nearly finished.'

'There's a note over there. By the door. A flyer or something.'

Ted picked up the piece of paper and read out loud:

Come to the harbour this Saturday evening and enjoy a special event. Funfair. Pony rides. Face painting and balloons. And at 8 p.m. a special ship from across the seas and across the centuries will visit our town to entertain and amaze one and all.

Ted gasped. 'Across the centuries! Suzie, do you see what's happening?'

'I don't know, Dad. Why don't you tell me?'

'It's a set-up. The pirates printed this. This way the whole village will be gathered at the harbour. All the easier to kidnap them in one fell swoop. It's an evil plot!'

Ted's ears were smoking.

'Dad, are you sure? You know, I've been thinking about Beasley and his whole story, and something about it doesn't make sense. And yesterday, after I fell –'

But Ted wasn't listening. He checked his watch. 'Half seven!' He leapt away from the table. 'Where's your mother? Where's JP? It's time for super power. We don't have a moment to lose!'

Half an hour later Suzie sat at her bedroom window, holding JP's telescope. The sky was overcast. The bay was empty. Her crutches lay crosswise on the bed. Asleep at the foot of the bed, Pucker snored and half-barked at dream uniforms.

The rest of the family had received their marching orders and headed into the evening. While Suzie stayed where she was. It was so unfair! And so stressful! Because how was she going to deal with what went wrong when she couldn't move?

And something always went wrong.

Below and to the right, where the sea waves crashed on the stony strand, Suzie saw flashes of fire. It was her dad, getting warmed up, getting ready to launch fireballs. But would he control them this time? Or would they fly off at odd angles and destroy schools and farmhouses?

Beyond the shoreline was a clump of trees outlined against the evening sky. In that little forest, Suzie knew, Clare sat at the base of a pine tree, hands on her temples, summoning forth her wave-making power. But what if the tidal wave brought other weather with it? Snow or hailstones? Or lightning bolts that would bring her sheltering tree crashing down, like the one that had crushed the Fiasco?

And what about Beasley? What was he up to? Suzie moved the telescope slowly across the horizon. No sign of the ship. No sign of Beasley. She panned back to the harbour. The townspeople had begun to gather. Shouts and laughter rang in the air and the lights of the funfair twinkled. All that was missing was the rumble of film music warning the audience that their world was about to fall apart.

And if Suzie had to come to the rescue, would her secret powers work at such a distance? She sighed. *Please*, she thought. *Please let it be over quickly*.

But wait a minute! Where was JP?

Across from the headland, beside the granite rocks where Pucker had dangled so precariously that morning, JP stood on the cliff edge, waving a stick like a sword and shouting across the abyss so he could hear his own echo.

'I believe I can fly.'

Can fly.

'I believe I can touch the sky.'

Touch the sky.

He tugged at his cape, assumed take-off position and looked at his watch. Five minutes to eight. Countdown time. He waited for the ship to appear. He knew his mission. Inclination angle. Rate of acceleration. The wind stirred, dark clouds bunched above Sherkin Island and, far below him, the sea began to swell. His mum was doing her job. He was ready to do his.

But what was that at his feet? An old gold coin?

Suzie was still trying to locate JP with the telescope when, from behind the headland, just as it had the day before, the pirate ship floated into view, the skull-and-crossbones flag flapping in the breeze. The crow's nest perched on the mizzenmast. Ranged along the landward deck were six cannon, ominously aimed at the town. Each cannon was manned by a pirate holding high a flaming torch. Ready to bombard the village, if they had to. Ready to kidnap.

Or were they? On the ship's deck, standing beside the sleepy-eyed, red-nosed captain was Beasley. A big smile on his face. As the ship moved closer to the harbour, Beasley pointed at the crowds of people. The captain nodded and they shook hands. Beasley jumped over the port rail and clambered down a rope ladder to a waiting motor boat. A hearty wave to the captain and off he sped. As Suzie watched his boat cut through the choppy water, three flashes of light came from a clump of bushes on the shore. Not the wood where Clare was, but a different one, further west. The boat shifted left and headed straight for the signal, bobbing lightly in the steadily rising waves.

Suzie waited. Time for JP to take off. Ted had it timed to the second. They had synchronised their watches. She checked the clock: 8:02. Waited. 8:03. And waited. Where *was* he?

*

JP sat on the ground, digging into the earth with the sharp end of his stick. Searching for buried treasure. Because if one coin could be found so easily, what riches might lie beneath? The measure trap had been right after all. Oh, where was Pucker when he needed him? Pucker the furious digger. A boy's best friend.

He dug steadily, dreaming of what he might buy with the gold. A year's supply of Curly Wurlys. A silk cape. A new collar for Pucker. Another Fiasco for his dad. A gardening shed for his mum. And for Suzie? Hmmm. An iPhone? Maybe. Or a book on pirates.

Pirates! He sprang to his feet. Out in the bay, torches blazing, cannon aimed, was the *Rabid Buffoon*, flag flying, sails billowing, prow cutting through the waves as it headed for the harbour with deadly intent. JP threw his stick aside, ran at full speed to the cliff edge and took off, arms extended, in full flight mode. But while he had been digging, his cape collar had rotated – and was now on back to front. So, as he flew, the force of the wind lifted the cape and wrapped it around his head. Was he going left or right? Up or down? He didn't know – he was flying blind! Cruising speed, optimum altitude, distraction potential – none of his dad's careful calculations mattered, because he had no idea where he was going.

Fizz, whang, whoosh. He screeched and flared across the violet sky like a comet. The corners of his cape flapped at his ears. He scratched and scrabbled at it until he finally cleared it from his face. But he was still blind! White blind? No, he was in the clouds. He pitched downwards. The wind whistled in his ears. Oh, why had he let himself be distracted by that stupid coin? 'Hold on, Dad,' he shouted into the cottony whiteness, 'I'm coming.'

He zipped out of the low-lying cloud, his eyes streaming with tears in the wind, desperately trying to figure out where he was. Top speed. Straight down. And suddenly there it was, the pirate ship, directly below him, its masts pointing skyward like giant spears. He saw that his approach was all wrong – a bad angle, too much pace, no control. He tried to curve outward but it was too late – he flew straight into the ship's rigging, like a football fired into goal.

While JP was thrashing about in the rigging, getting more and more tangled, Suzie was watching Beasley, who was halfway to shore in his motor boat. He was rubbing his hands together and laughing wildly, head tossed back. Beyond him was another, smaller boat, heading toward him as if to rendezvous but having problems with the rising waves. She looked closely at the second boat. Fitzhugh at the helm! Though it was a wreck on the outside, there was a glint of gold behind its dull windows. Suzie trained her X-ray vision on the weathered bow: beneath she saw gold, silver, Connemara marble. So *they* were the thieves! The Powers had been playing into Beasley's hands. He had set the whole thing up! He had created a big free-for-all with pirates and a big ship so that the Powers would get involved and tie up the guards and allow him to get away – the evil genius!

But the waves grew wilder, keeping Beasley and Fitzhugh's boats apart. Yellow lightning forked brilliantly from sky to sea. Suzie returned her attention to the pirate ship. The skull and crossbones snapped in the breeze. The deck rocked in the bad weather and the captain looked confused. Trying to keep on their feet, the pirates grabbed rails or rigging. Her dad's plan was working. So where were the fireballs?

And why were the pirates pointing at the sky?

The sky! They were pointing at JP! There he was, wrapped in the ship's rigging just below the crow's nest. Caught like a fly in a web.

A loud explosion came from the beach, and the first of Ted's fireballs flew skyward, missing the ship by a wide margin and falling into the sea with a hiss. Suzie saw Ted running along the strand, hopping from one foot to another, his head in a cloud of smoke. She concentrated. *Not now, Dad. Not now!*

JP dangled from the rigging, upside down, his head resting on the edge of the mainsail. The more he struggled, the more tangled he got. As the ship rocked and the masts swayed back and forth, he grew sick to his stomach. Far below he could see the pirates pointing at him. A couple of them were trying to get on the rigging to climb up to him, but they couldn't get a grip in the turmoil. What could he do? He felt like throwing up.

A loud explosion, a flash of heat and a fireball hit the crow's nest, which ignited with a roar. Bound and helpless, JP looked up at the spilling sparks and hungry flames. 'Suzie!' he shouted. 'Dad! Mum! Help me!' Burning embers fell on the mainsail, setting it alight. The fire gobbled up the sail, getting closer and closer to his head. And the pirates – the pirates were trying to *help* him. 'We're coming,' one of them shouted in his funny

accent. 'We'll save you!' But the wind was too strong for them. His mum had done it this time. Gale-force winds. Ten-metre waves. And rain everywhere except where it was needed – on the burning sail. *Is this it?* he thought. *Is this the end?*

'Pucker! Help me, Pucker!'

Ever so faintly, Suzie could hear JP crying. Pucker, with his super doggie hearing, had jumped onto the bed and was staring at the ship, whining and growling. The fireballs kept flying. The waves grew wilder. Something had to be done.

It was Suzie's time. This was the girl who could read *The Hobbit* in a day, speak Spanish to visiting students, create origami birds of advanced design. Who wanted more than anything to lead an ordinary life. And yet who, when it had to be done, could save her family.

As she had when sending the mental message to her mother, or saving Pucker and JP on the ledge, she bent all her energy in the direction of the ship. The fire – before she did anything else she needed to douse the fire. Fiercely concentrating, she slowly moved the rain squall across the sky, until it was directly above the burning sail. She doubled, trebled, quadrupled the rain flow, until the fire was out. Next, she calmed the winds. The pirates, back on their feet, scampered up the rigging and unwound the boy from the knots of smoking rope.

So JP was safe. Now – what about the *real* villains?

As the winds calmed, Beasley had been able to negotiate his motor boat alongside the treasure craft. He jumped aboard, pushed Fitzhugh off the wheel and headed them out to sea.

'OK, Pucker,' Suzie said, 'let's see how Mr Beasley likes this!'

She funnelled a wave, small but powerful, at the boat. It created a whirlpool, so that the boat circled and circled, going nowhere. Then she let a blast of wind gradually push the boat back towards the cove. Beasley, she could see, was puzzled. Then, as he realised what was happening, he flew into a rage. They were going backwards. He pounded the steering wheel with his fists. Took off his yachting cap and smacked Fitzhugh on the head and upraised arms.

'Hah!' Suzie said to Pucker. 'He isn't laughing now.'

She rang the police on Ted's mobile.

'Crimestoppers,' a guard answered.

'Hello. This is Clare Power.'

A pause at the other end. Would they believe they were talking to her mother?

'Hello?' Suzie said.

'Mrs Power, what can I do for you? We're very busy here at the station. A crisis on our hands, as I'm sure you're aware.'

'Guard, that's why I'm ringing. To reassure you.'

'Ah.'

'I know it looks like my husband and I are making a mess of things out here.'

''Twouldn't be the first time,' the guard muttered.

'But it's only a diversion.'

'So *that's* what it is. The owners of the tall ship might not agree.'

'Guard, listen to me. There's a small motor boat with blue trim about to founder in the small cove north of town, across from the island.'

'Yes?'

'What with the waves and all, I'm worried about the safety of the crew.'

'Are you now?'

'Oh,' Suzie said, 'and if you happen to look in the boat's hold, I believe you'll find some stolen goods. Some *very valuable* stolen goods.'

She hung up. The pirate ship was drifting peacefully, no worse for wear, bar the shattered crow's nest and a burnt sail. From the harbour came the cheers of villagers, who had been watching JP's rescue. Clare and Ted were together on the shore, beaming as if *they* had plucked their son from the burning mast. The clouds had cleared and the sky stretched pale and milky above the island. All was tranquil except for the whirlpool sending Beasley and Fitzhugh into the arms of the guards.

Suzie laid the telescope on the floor. 'Pucker-stucker, I have a headache.'

He jumped on to the bed and licked her face.

'Good doggie,' she said.

She felt better already.

12

Who'll Stop the Rain

'To the left a little. Back a bit. Say *cheese*.'

The Powers stood on the steps of the Baltimore Garda station, arms linked, smiling for the camera. To the side, stern-faced and nervous, were the mayor of the town and the Garda sergeant.

The camera flashed. The reporter from the local newspaper asked Ted how it felt to be a hero.

Ted stepped forward, basking in the glory, pretending the attention was nothing. 'We came to Baltimore for a holiday,' he said, as if addressing a class. 'And frankly, we needed a break. No powers, we said. But when your country needs you, what choice do you have but to answer the call?' He shrugged and grinned.

Leaning on her crutches, Suzie rolled her eyes.

Nudged by the sergeant, the mayor spoke up. 'On behalf of all the citizens of Baltimore,' she said, 'I extend a warm, hearty thank you to the Powers for helping us to apprehend the criminals who stole so many Irish treasures, including our own beloved Cross of Ballyuseless. The robbers are now in gaol, and the cross has been restored to its former glory in Feckless Abbey.'

Half-hearted applause from the small crowd. Muffled howls from Pucker, who was locked in the car and had wild red eyes and bared yellow teeth trained on the sergeant.

'And as a gesture of our profound appreciation,' the mayor continued quickly, 'the town of Baltimore is delighted to make available to the Powers – to replace their car unfortunately destroyed by, ahem, high winds – the loan of a

brand new Chrysler Catastrophe to get you on your way to Dublin without delay.'

The crowd looked at the new car, which was rocking back and forth with the force of Pucker's howling uniform-rage.

'We only do what we have to,' Ted said, 'to protect Ireland and its people. It is our destiny, because we are –'

He looked at JP

'Pooper-soured!' JP shouted.

Ted grimaced. 'Yes, well. You all know what he means. But seriously, we would be delighted to stay on here in Baltimore for another day or two if –'

'No, no, no,' the sergeant said loudly, waving his hands in the air. 'You've done more than enough for us already. Please go. Now.'

Half an hour later, the Powers were on the road. The Garda sergeant, limping back to the station house and nursing a nasty Pucker-bite, said to the mayor, 'I thought they'd never leave.'

'What about the lawsuit that the tall-ship owners are bringing against the town?'

'That's your problem,' he said. 'I have to go to the doctor and get this bleeding leg stitched up.'

He stopped and looked at the dark skies. Bad weather, the forecast said, was on its way from Dublin.

He shook his head. 'The Powers. What did I ever do to deserve them?'

The Catastrophe ran like a Swiss watch.

'Can we get one of these cars, Dad?' JP asked.

'I don't know. You know me. Always more comfortable with a Fiasco.'

'I think we've had enough fiascos,' Suzie said from the back seat. 'And as for catastrophes ...'

Clare looked at Suzie in the rear-view mirror. 'Cynicism, young lady, is no attitude to have on a beautiful summer's day.'

Suzie looked out the window. It was lashing rain.

'You can't save the kitchen,' Clare continued, sounding like Ted, 'without breaking a few dishes. And just because –'

'I know,' Suzie said, 'just because I don't have any powers.'

Suzie returned to her book. She had finished *Treasure Island* and was on to *Kidnapped*. Clare rolled her eyes.

At Mitchelstown they stopped for petrol. When Ted was paying, the attendant asked him where they were headed.

'Dublin.'

'Drive carefully now.'

'Will do.'

'And mind the flooding.'

'Flooding?'

The road to Castlerock was closed. In fact there was no road. It had turned into a river. The Powers' car was met outside the town by members of the army. They were sandbagging people's houses and rescuing residents who had retreated to their roofs.

An officer approached the car. More Pucker-mania in the back seat.

Ignoring the howls, Ted asked, 'What's the problem, soldier?' His voice had dropped an octave. It was his I'm-here-to-save-the-day voice.

'Corporal Quinn, actually.' The corporal looked at the family warily. At Pucker bouncing around behind the back seat like a pinball. 'You live in Castlerock?'

'We do.'

'And aren't you – ?'

'We are.'

Rain dripped from the corporal's hat onto Ted's arm. 'Ah. Yes. Well, you'd better find a hotel for this evening. You see, we're moving people out, not sending them back in.'

'Not sending *ordinary* people back in,' Ted said. 'If there's a problem, we're here to serve.'

'Oh, there's a problem all right.'

Ted did not like the man's tone. 'And what might that be?'

'It's as if a certain superhero family thought they could control the weather. So, who knows how much longer we're in for this mess.'

'Mum,' JP shouted, 'you set the weather, remember?'

Clare cleared her throat. 'Ah, Ted?'

Ted didn't answer. Sparks were crackling under his collar. 'I'm sure you're wrong,' he said to the corporal.

'Why don't we let the International Superhero Association be the judge of that?'

Ted bristled. Suzie looked up from her book and wrinkled her brow. At once the rain stopped, the clouds cleared and the sun burst forth.

'Well, would you look at that,' the corporal said, looking skyward. 'Wonders never cease. Still and all, it'll be a while before all this water subsides.'

'We can't just –'

'On your way, sir.'

'But we're the –'

'I said, on your way.'

Ted backed up and turned around. Wreathed in smoke, trembling with wild barking, the car drove off in the opposite direction, a Catastrophe in search of yet another disaster.

The End